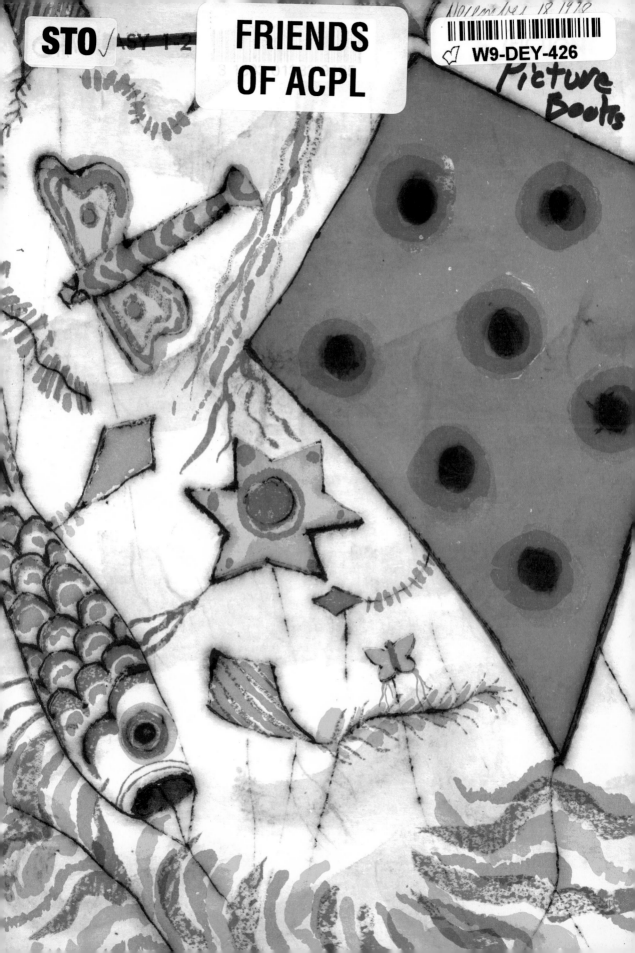

Picture
Book

THE
BATTLE OF
REUBEN ROBIN
&
KITE UNCLE JOHN

story by Mary Calhoun
pictures by Janet McCaffery

William Morrow & Company ● New York 1973

Calhoun, Mary.
The battle of Reuben Robin and Kite Uncle John.

SUMMARY: A nest-building robin is as determined to
take Uncle John's kite string as Uncle John is to keep it.
[1. Robins—Stories. 2. Kites—Fiction]
I. McCaffery, Janet, illus. [E] II. Title.
PZ7.C1278 Bat 72-12947
ISBN 0-688-20075-3
ISBN 0-688-30075-8 (lib. bdg.)

Talk about your bold, sassy robins!
Let me tell you about the time
Kite Uncle John met the boldest,
most bound-determined robin of them all.
Now all the young'uns
called the old man Kite Uncle John,
because he taught them
how to fly their kites.

He was a patient man.
It takes patience to build a kite.
It takes patience to fly a kite,
to catch the wind just right.
Well, one March,
Kite Uncle John patiently hunted
until he found
just the right kite string,
smooth as silk and strong as steel.

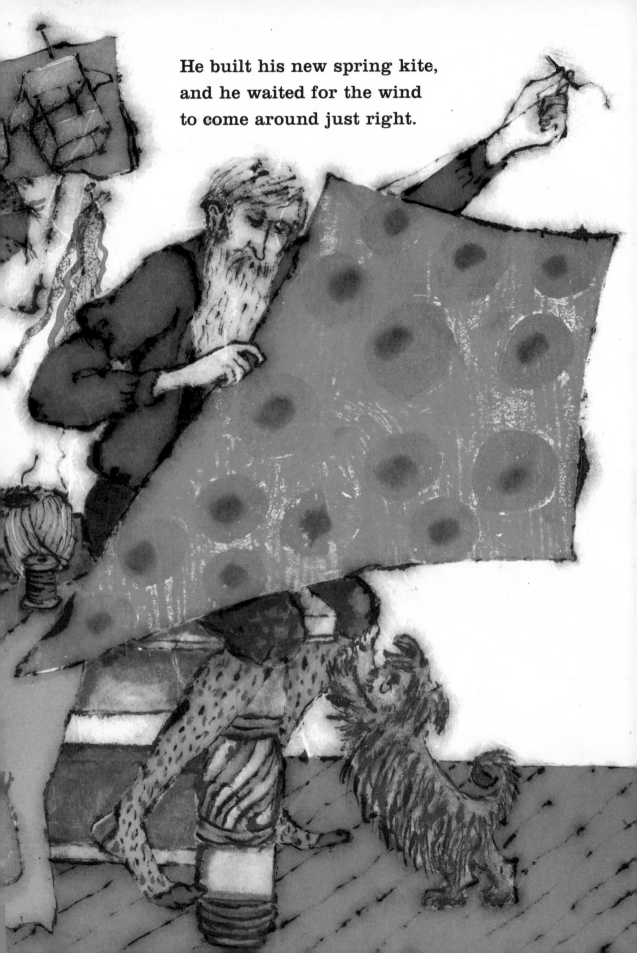

He built his new spring kite,
and he waited for the wind
to come around just right.

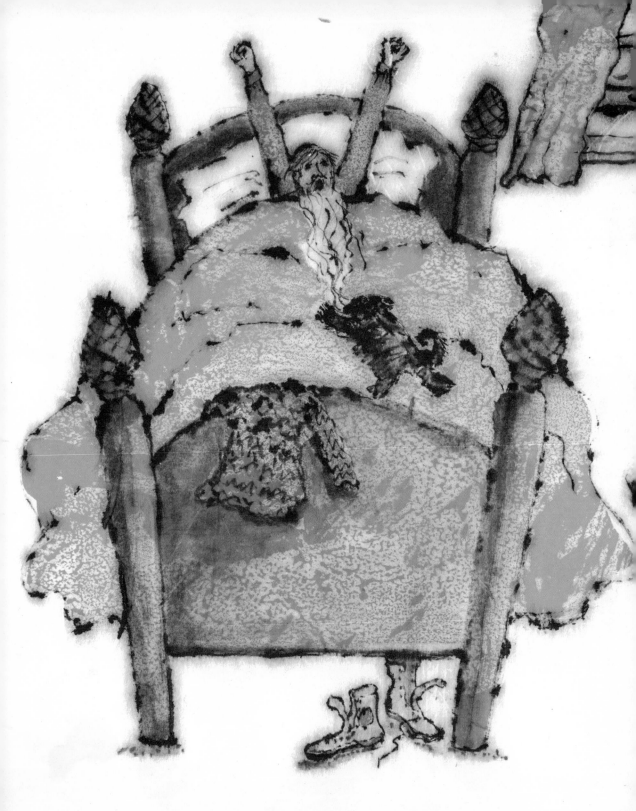

One morning he woke up and heard
the wind frisking around the eaves.
"Just right!" he cried.
"The very best day for flying a kite!"

He pulled on his clothes
and reached to the windowsill,
where he'd laid his ball of kite string.

Gone!
His fine, strong string was gone!
He looked out the window,
and there was his kite string,
slithering up a tree.
Into a nest.
A couple of robins had stolen his string.
The wife bird
had a mud-and-twig framework started,
and she was just a-working away,
busy tucking string into her nest.
The man bird stood by on a branch,
putting in a poke with his beak
and chirping proudly,
the robber, for sure.
Kite Uncle John tore out of the house,
and his white beard blew in the wind.

He shinnied up the tree,
with the robins flapping around his ears,
squawking.
"I'll just unravel your nest, Reuben!"
he said to that fat man robin.
"Teach you to go a-thieving!"
Laughing, he pulled his kite string
down from the nest.
Mad?
Say, that Reuben Robin screeched up a clack
like Uncle John had stolen
his first-born son!
That hot-headed robin hopped and squawked
and flew in to nip at the string.
Kite Uncle John
only brushed him off patiently,
got his kite from the back porch,
and set off for his kite-flying hill.

But Reuben Robin was bound-determined
to have that string,
the very best
nest-building string he'd seen,
smooth as silk and strong as steel.
Swooping and screeching,
he followed Kite Uncle John up the hill,
tree branch to fence post,
scolding all the way,
telling the old man
what a rotten homebreaker he was.
He didn't know the meaning of fear,
that robin.
He just wanted Uncle John's string.
Kite Uncle John
didn't yell at the bird, though.
He was a patient man,
and he figured the robin
would give up and go away.

His beard rippled pretty in the wind
as he got set to fly his kite.
He ran down the hill
and caught the updraft in his kite.
He let go, she dipped,
he played out string, and up she sailed.
Uncle John's kite was on the wind!
Through the string in his hand
he could feel the kite
tugging and pulling away, eager to fly.
Easy, he let out the string,
smooth as silk.

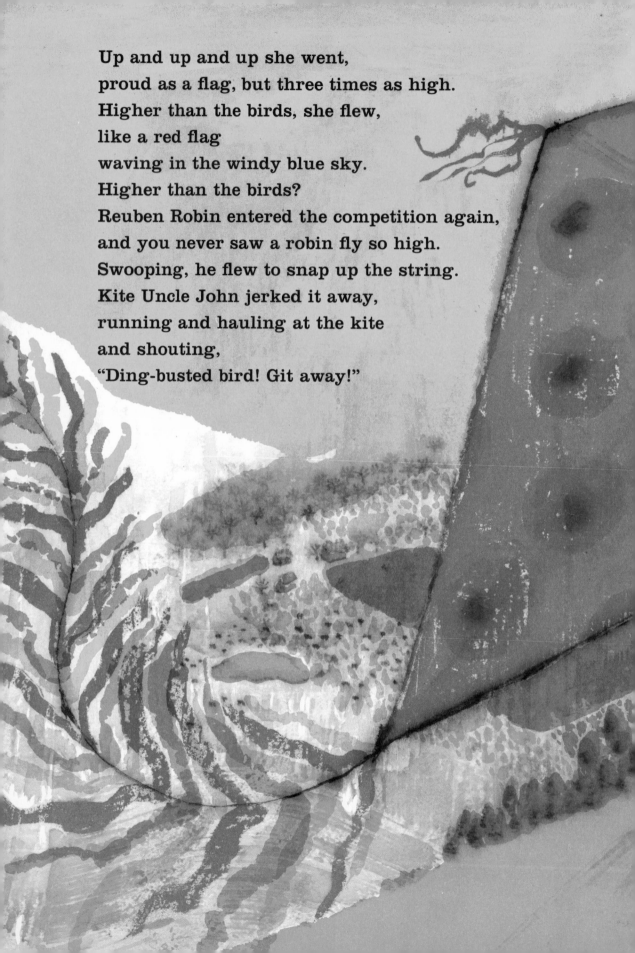

Up and up and up she went,
proud as a flag, but three times as high.
Higher than the birds, she flew,
like a red flag
waving in the windy blue sky.
Higher than the birds?
Reuben Robin entered the competition again,
and you never saw a robin fly so high.
Swooping, he flew to snap up the string.
Kite Uncle John jerked it away,
running and hauling at the kite
and shouting,
"Ding-busted bird! Git away!"

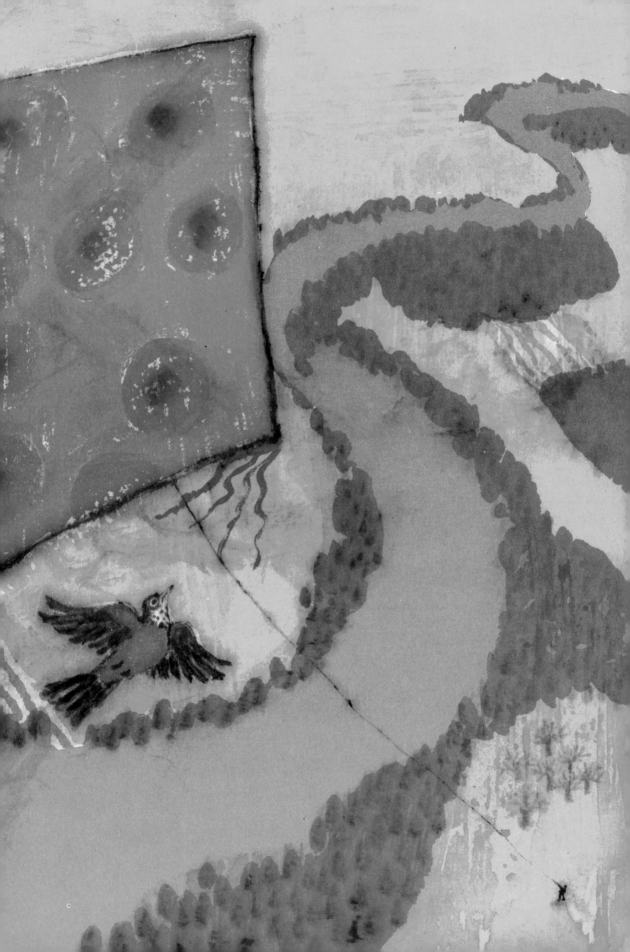

But that was just the start of the battle
between Reuben Robin and Kite Uncle John
on that kite-flying day.
Next that smart-aleck bird
gave one powerful beat of his wings.
He sailed up above the kite.
And <u>sat</u> on it.
That infernal robin
sat right down on Uncle John's kite
and rode the wind.

But not for long.
The kite began to drop
because of the added weight.

About that time
Uncle John lost a little of his patience.
"Confound you, bird!
I'll fry you for supper!" he shouted.
He gave a smart jerk to the kite
and unseated Reuben.
Then he ran like a filly
to get the kite up again,
with the bird barreling along
right after the string.

Kite Uncle John was a sight to see,
that day on the hill,
white beard whisking in the breeze
as he dashed and danced and doubled back.
He ran every which way with that kite,

playing out string,

pulling it in again.

Reuben swooped at the string;
Uncle John hauled it away.

Reuben snatched with his beak;
Uncle John twitched the kite just in time.
The kite started to fall;

then the wind caught it up again.
Reuben, he screeched and flapped,
grabbing at the string with his claws,
pecking at it with his beak.
"Never saw a bird so bound-determined!"
gasped Uncle John.

Reuben Robin grabbed the string
with his beak
and flew away with the kite.
Uncle John pulled,
and the bird flapped as hard as he could,
trying not to give way,
tugging at his end of the string.
But Kite Uncle John was stronger.
Bit by bit, he reeled in the bird.

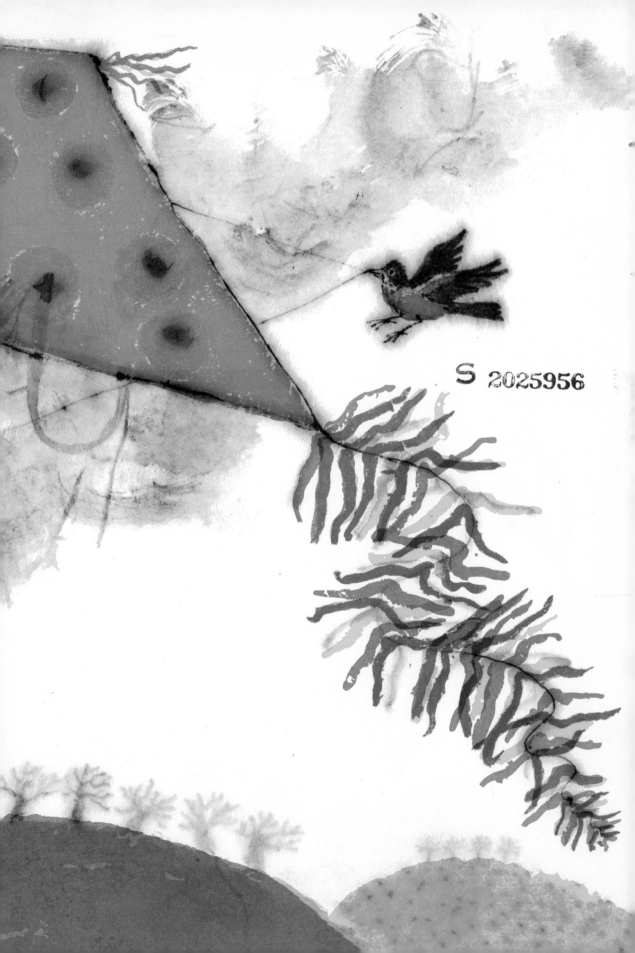

Still flapping,
feet braced against nothing,
Reuben Robin came skidding down the sky.

Then Kite Uncle John
found his patience again.
When the bird was only
five feet above his head,
still hanging onto the string,
Uncle John threw something white
in the air.
"Here you are, Reuben.
Try this instead!" he called.
And what do you know!
The robin let go of the kite string
and darted to catch the white thing.
It was a piece of Uncle John's beard.
He'd grabbed out
a tuft of his own white beard.
Well, if there's anything
a robin would prize
to build into his nest,
it's a bit of soft fluff.
Reuben caught that hair on the wing,
like a bug.

Then he made to go back for the string.
Yet Kite Uncle John was a patient man.
He pulled out another tuft of his beard.
"Ouch! Here!"
And Reuben Robin caught it up, too.
He was some really smart bird,
for he didn't lose
the first piece of beard.

Then he took off for home like a shot
with his two tufts of beard.
Patient Uncle John
was rid of that pestiferous bird.
But only until
next kite-flying, nest-building season.

Next March, there came Reuben,
bound-determined,
begging for a fluff of hair.
Uncle John was a patient man,
so he gave the bird a bit of beard.
And he gave his beard
and he flew his kites
every March for the rest of his life.